The Charms of US Farms

Finding Out How Things Work

Book 1

Written by Raven Howell

Illustrated by Ann Pilicer

The Charms of US Farms
Finding Out How Things Work
Book 1
Written by Raven Howell
Illustrated by Ann Pilicer
Graphic Design by Tara Sizemore
Published October 2025
Skippy Creek
Imprint of Jan-Carol Publishing, Inc.

This is a work of fiction. Any resemblance to actual people, either living or dead is entirely coincidental. All names, characters, and events are the product of the author's imagination.

This book may not be reproduced in whole or part, in any manner whatsoever, without written permission, with the exception of brief quotations within book reviews or articles.

Copyright © Raven Howell
ISBN: 978-1-970471-05-2
Library of Congress Control Number: On file

You may contact the publisher:
Jan-Carol Publishing, Inc.
PO Box 701
Johnson City, TN 37605
publisher@jancarolpublishing.com
www.jancarolpublishing.com

Chapters

1. Early Classroom Chatter 1
2. Ms. Della Dishes Dates 5
3. Crops and Cattle 8
4. Terrific Tractors 11
5. How Corny! 13
6. Next Stop: Farmer Dole 17
7. Cows Have How Many Stomachs? 21
8. What Does Baseball Have to Do With It? 25
9. What Did You Learn? 29
10. Billy's "Home Run" 31

About the Author 35

Chapter 1
Early Classroom Chatter

Sophia's hand shoots up. "Ms. Miller, I'm excited about our class trip to the farmland!"

Next to her, Delilah tucks her notebook into her book bag and yawns, adding, "I am, too, but will anybody on the farm be awake at this early time in the morning?"

"They sure are!" responds Ms. Miller cheerfully, packing up her own bag. "Farms wake up with the sunrise just as they have for thousands of years." She adds, "A farmer's work is hard. They work long hours, sometimes from sunrise to sunset."

Although this fact surprises the students, Billy grumbles, "But what makes farmland so different anyway?"

Ms. Miller smiles. "Some of us have yards with gardens. Some of us enjoy parks to walk through and play in, but farmland is special—it feeds us and clothes us."

Billy rolls his eyes and mutters, "How can that be possible?"

Ms. Miller continues, "Hundreds of years ago, most American families lived on farms and raised crops and animals to feed and clothe themselves. Now we don't have as many farms, but this smaller number of farms produces more."

Billy remains grouchy but lines up with the other eager students as everyone climbs into the bus for the day's trip.

Chapter 2

Ms. Della Dishes Dates

During the bus ride, Ms. Miller announces, "First, we'll visit Ms. Della's farm where we'll learn about corn. Then we'll meet Farmer Dole and visit with his cows and cotton fields."

Soon, the bus chugs up a hill on a long, winding driveway. After the bus is parked, a perky Ms. Della rushes out of her house to meet everyone. She waves the students into her large kitchen, "Welcome to the farm!"

Ms. Della offers the children drinks and her home-baked date cake. Everyone says thank you. Growing quiet, they enjoy delicious bites while Ms. Della explains the reason she is sharing her date cake.

"Farms first started being used with the growing of wheat and barley. Also popular with farmers at the time were jujube, a red date, and quite the funny name for a fruit!" The students giggle, agreeing.

Madison asks, "What happened on the farms after the planting of the grains?"

Chapter 3

Crops and Cattle

"Cattle soon joined the farm: sheep, goats and pigs, and then other animals," says Ms. Della. "These and other crops and animals were domesticated. That means they were being grown or raised in a controlled process that made providing for people easier."

"Today's farms produce many different plants and animals that are used for food and other products all around the world."

To explain this further, Ms. Della grins at Juanita. "Some farmers grow common plants for making clothing, such as ramie, cotton, and flax. I bet you have a favorite shirt."

Juanita nods and says, "I sure do!"

    Then Ms. Della asks Tyler, "Dairy farming produces dairy products for us. Do you find a cookie yummier if it's dunked in a glass of milk?"

    Tyler gives a big smile, "How did you know that, Ms. Della?"

    The students laugh, all agreeing with Tyler that a cookie is definitely yummier with a glass of mlk, and yes, they enjoy scoops of ice cream, too.

    Ms. Miller tells her students, "We enjoy all these things because of farms and farmers like Ms. Della and Farmer Dole."

Chapter 4
Terrific Tractors

The group gathers on the wide front porch of the farmhouse where Ms. Della's young children have toy chests full of tractors and trucks, tiny versions of the best sources of power for farms.

Ms. Della's bright eyes sparkle. "I'm proud of our farmland. We've come a long way from using wooden ploughs, cutting with sickles, and sowing seeds by hand. Today, most believe you can't be a farmer if you don't have a tractor. They pull plows, power planters, and guide tillage equipment."

"Come, let's take a look!" she says, guiding everyone down the path under the bright blue, sunny sky.

Chapter 5

How Corny!

Ms. Della points to the cornfields. "Corn is the most important US crop. Like all farmers, I plant corn in springtime. Before it's harvested in autumn, corn stalks can grow up to 20 feet tall!"

Then she says, "The next time you use your crayons, paints, or paper, think of the farmers who grow and tend to corn. Many products we all use every day have corn, including these."

The students are surprised by this and chatter amongst themselves as everyone treks back to the school bus. Their morning had gone by quickly and now they were ready for their next visit with Farmer Dole. The visitors cheerfully wave goodbye to Ms. Della from the bus windows.

Billy, though, appears a bit bored and slides down in his seat when the bus roars back down the long, winding driveway.

Chapter 6

Next Stop: Farmer Dole

A little while later, arriving at Farmer Dole's farm, the children jump out of the bus as, unexpectedly, friendly dogs are the first ones to greet them! The farmer himself is not far behind.

Farmer Dole, wearing a brown hat and removing his work gloves, calls out, "Hello, hello!" and pleasantly greets the group.

He informs the visitors that one of the dogs helps to move the livestock on the farm, and the other is a guardian dog. The guardian dog protects some of the farm animals from predators.

He directs the class to the large, open barn and says, "We name our cats and dogs, but did you know that almost half of all farmers name their cows as well? Researchers have found that cows with names end up producing more milk than those who aren't named."

The children gather around the open stalls as Farmer Dole points to his favorite cow.

Chapter 7

Cows Have How Many Stomachs?

"This cow especially likes to be petted and scratched behind her ears. Her name is Bessie. What would you name your cow if you had one?"

As Farmer Dole takes the class outside in the cool afternoon air, he says, "Scientific studies show that over the years the amount of meat and products that cows and other animals produce has increased."

Then he chuckles and adds, "By the way, I bet you didn't know a cow has four stomachs!"

He gives a wink and looks at the students.

"If your stomach rumbles when you're hungry, can you imagine how a cow may be feeling?"

Sophia wonders out loud, "Would that be four times the rumbling?"

And the other students join in the conversation, laughing.

Chapter 8

What Does Baseball Have to Do With It?

As they hike to Farmer Dole's cotton fields, the farmer explains, "The southern half of the United States farms the most amount of cotton, an area called 'The Cotton Belt.' In the year 1793, Eli Whitney invented the cotton gin, a machine that pulls seeds from cotton bolls and made the production of cotton much easier."

The students consider Farmer Dole's words, yet Billy doesn't seem to pay much attention as he absently kicks a rock on the ground.

Noticing the athletic cap Billy is wearing, Farmer Dole asks Billy his favorite sport. Now interested, Billy looks up. "It's baseball!" he says. And quicker than a wink, Farmer Dole pulls a baseball from his pocket. With a gentle toss, he throws it into Billy's hands. Billy catches it.

"Wow! You're like a magician who pulls rabbits out of a hat!" Billy says with a smirk.

Farmer Dole chuckles again. "I've always enjoyed playing baseball, too." Then he leans forward saying, "Did you know 150 yards of cotton are in just one regulation baseball?"

Billy's eyes grow wide. "That's a lot of cotton for a small ball!"

After that, with Farmer Dole insisting Billy keep the old baseball, Ms. Miller and the children give their thanks and make their way to the bus once again.

Chapter 9

What Did You Learn?

While the students grow quiet on the drive back to school from a long day, Ms. Miller asks the children what they learned from their school trip.

From the front seat, Juanita says, "I learned that groceries don't just come from a market, but they're produced by farmers!"

Tyler adds, "I know I'll be writing my report about Eli Whitney who invented the cotton gin. I want to be an inventor, too, and help keep our environment healthy and clean."

Delilah happily announces that she would name her cow "Moo" if lucky enough to have one some day.

Chapter 10
Billy's "Home Run"

Ms. Miller glances at Billy, who has been looking thoughtfully out the bus window. "Billy, did you like the farm trip? What did you learn today?"

Finally, Billy breaks into a wide, toothy grin and says, "I learned that I want to be a farmer when I grow up!" The students all clap and Tyler gives his friend a high five.

But it's Sophia's hand that shoots up again. "Yes, Sophia?" Ms. Miller asks.

"I was inspired to write a poem about the day." Sophia clears her throat, and looking at her notebook, reads:

"Farmland is cattle-d,
It's seeded and ploughed,
Hooray for the cotton, the corn,
And the cow!"

"That's wonderful, Sophia!" exclaims Ms. Miller. "I wonder what you'll write for our next school trip…"

Author's Note

My hope is that this book may instigate a spark for children of all ages to become increasingly aware of what our land and our natural world offers us in our daily lives. With this awareness comes regard, and from there, motivation sprouts to treat the earth in all of her beauty with tender, loving care.

About the Author

Raven Howell is a children's book and magazine writer. Her books have won several awards including Excellence in Children's Literature, and the Literary Global Award.

She is the Director of *Kids Corner*, and Publishing and Creative Advisor with *Red Clover Reader*. Raven writes children's educational books and is a contributing author for *Reading is Fundamental SoCal*.

🌐 www.ravenhowell.com
📷 atpearthkeeper

www.ingramcontent.com/pod-product-compliance
Lightning Source LLC
Jackson TN
JSHW082134291025
93367JS00019B/141